For my dear friends Shirley, Lily, Francis
and Queston, who make my trips to
Hong Kong exciting and memorable.

Neil x

Red Robin Books is an imprint of Corner To Learn Limited

Published by

Corner To Learn Limited
Willow Cottage • 26 Purton Stoke • Swindon • Wiltshire SN5 4JF • UK

ISBN: 978-1-908702-11-1

First published in the UK 2014
Text © Neil Griffiths 2014
Illustrations © Peggy Collins 2014

Design by David Rose

Printed in China

Scaredy Bear

Neil Griffiths

Illustrated by
Peggy Collins

Baby bear had been born on a soft bed of straw and leaves, inside a dark cave. This is where he had stayed for all his young life and he liked it there.

Sometimes he got a little scared when he heard strange noises or saw shadows.

But he always had his
mum to cuddle and that
made him feel better.

But now he was big and brave enough to go out on his first adventure, into the outside world.

Well he was, with a little
encouragement from his mum.

The first thing he saw was a fresh flower and he decided to smell it with his wet nose.

He was just about to take a big sniff when...

Oh dear, scaredy bear, it's
only a cute caterpillar.
Do come out of hiding!

Baby bear then spotted his first cool pool of fresh
water and decided to take a drink with his long tongue.
He was just about to take a little sip when...

Oh dear, scaredy bear, it's only a tiny turtle.
Do come out of hiding!

Baby bear then saw his first shiny
nut and decided to crack it open
with his sharp teeth. He was just
about to take a bite when...

Oh dear, scaredy bear,
it's only an old owl.
Do come out of hiding!

Baby bear then found his first wriggly worm
and decided to touch it with his soft paw.
He was just about to tickle it when...

Oh dear, scaredy bear, its only a friendly frog. Do come out of hiding!

Baby bear then heard his first cricket and
decided to get closer with his furry ears.
He was just about to
listen to it when...

Oh dear, scaredy bear, it's only
a slithering grass snake.
Do come out of hiding!

Baby bear then saw his first dark cave from the outside
and decided to peer inside with his bright brown eyes.
He was just about to peer in when...

Oh dear, baby bear, there's no need to be scared. Do come out of hiding. Look, it's only mummy bear!

Baby bear stopped being scared and was glad he had his *mum* to cuddle tightly again, which always made him feel better.